Gus Grows a Plant

Gus Grows a Plant

by Frank Remkiewicz

Cartwheel
B·O·O·K·S ®

SCHOLASTIC INC.

New York   Toronto   London   Auckland
Sydney   Mexico City   New Delhi   Hong Kong

For Donna

Copyright © 2012 by Frank Remkiewicz

All rights reserved. Published by Scholastic Inc.
SCHOLASTIC and associated logos are
trademarks and/or registered trademarks of Scholastic Inc.
Lexile is a registered trademark of MetaMetrics, Inc.

Library of Congress Cataloging-in-Publication Data is available.

ISBN 978-0-545-34052-6

12 11 10 9 8   16 17/0

Printed in the U.S.A.   40
First printing, March 2012

Spring is here.

Time to plant.

Gus gets seeds.

Dad digs.

Gus digs, too.

Gus plants a seed.

The seed needs water.

Soon Gus has a plant.

The plant has a worm.

The plant needs sun.

It needs more water.

And fresh air.

The plant grows.

And grows.

How big is it?

Very big.

Bigger than Gus.

Wait!

Gus has an idea.

Gus grows, too!